THE ZACK FILES™

Elvis the Turnip...and Me

By Dan Greenburg

Illustrated by Jack E. Davis

GROSSET & DUNLAP • NEW YORK

I'd like to thank my editors,
Jane O'Connor and Judy Donnelly,
who make the process of writing and revising
so much fun, and without whom
these books would not exist.

I also want to thank Catherine Daly,
Jennifer Dussling, and Laura Driscoll
for their terrific ideas.

Text copyright © 1998 by Dan Greenburg. Illustrations copyright © 1998 by Jack E. Davis. All rights reserved. Published by Grosset & Dunlap, Inc., a member of Penguin Putnam Books for Young Readers, New York. THE ZACK FILES is a trademark of The Putnam & Grosset Group. GROSSET & DUNLAP is a trademark of Grosset & Dunlap, Inc. Published simultaneously in Canada. Printed in the U.S.A.

Library of Congress Cataloging-in-Publication Data
Greenburg, Dan.
    Elvis the turnip...and me / by Dan Greenburg ; illustrated by Jack E. Davis.
      p. cm. — (The Zack files)
    Summary: Late one night when ten-year-old Zack hears strains of "You Ain't Nothin' but a Hound Dog" coming from the refrigerator, he discovers the possibility that Elvis lives on as a turnip.
    [1. Turnips—Fiction. 2. Supernatural—Fiction.] I. Davis, Jack E., ill. II. Title III. Series: Greenburg, Dan. Zack files.
PZ7.G8278El 1998
[Fic]—dc21
                                    98-3988
                                       CIP

ISBN 0-448-41749-9   M N O P Q R S T   AC

Chapter 1

Has anything ever talked to you that wasn't a person? Out loud, I mean.

Two things have talked to me so far. A cat and a turnip. When I was in Florida, two dolphins talked to me. But that was by ESP and not out loud, so it doesn't count.

The cat who talked to me was in an animal shelter in New York. He turned out to be my great-grandfather, Maurice, who died and came back as a cat. The turnip I'll tell you about in a minute. But first I should say who I am and all that stuff.

OK. My name is Zack. I'm ten and a half, and I go to the Horace Hyde-White School for Boys. That's in New York City, by the way. My mom and dad are divorced, and I spend half my time with each of them. I was at my dad's apartment when the thing with the turnip started.

I woke up in the middle of the night. I was really hungry. Dad had been on a real health kick for the past couple weeks. Just that day he'd gone out and bought a whole lot of vegetables. Some of the vegetables were ones I hadn't even seen before. I'm not too crazy about vegetables, if you want to know the truth. Especially the kind Dad buys. I think I'm too old to try getting used to vegetables I haven't even seen before.

Dinner was a wheat-germ burger, a sprout salad, and carrot juice. I was starved for some real food. A couple of chocolate chip cookies and a bottle of Dr. Pepper was what I wanted.

I tiptoed out of my room and into the kitchen. I could practically taste those chocolate chip cookies. I didn't care if they weren't healthy. I'll have plenty of time to be healthy when I'm old.

I got the cookies. Then I opened the refrigerator door to get the soda. That's when I heard it. Singing. Singing from inside the vegetable bin.

It kind of freaked me out, if you want to know the truth. I mean, the last thing you want to hear coming from inside your vegetable bin is singing. The song coming from the vegetable bin was "You Ain't Nothin' but a Hound Dog." How could something small enough to fit inside a vegetable bin sing anything? I had to find out what it was. But instead of opening the vegetable bin, I closed the refrigerator door.

I wasn't afraid to see what it was. I just wasn't ready yet. Sometimes, if you're going to do something like find out what's in your vegetable bin, singing "You Ain't Nothin' but a Hound Dog," you have to kind of ease into it. You don't want to rush it. If you rushed it, you might scare whatever was singing. You wouldn't want to do that. If you scare a wild animal, it might attack you. Especially if it's doing something like singing "You Ain't Nothin' but a Hound Dog."

I didn't know what to do. Part of me really wanted to see what it was. Part of me didn't want to scare it. What would I do if it attacked me? What could I use to defend myself?

I turned on the kitchen light. I noticed a large frying pan hanging on the wall. I

picked it up and crept back to the refrigerator.

Slowly, slowly, I opened the refrigerator
door.

Slowly, slowly, I slid open the vegetable
bin.

The singing was louder than ever. But
there was nothing in the vegetable bin except vegetables: tomatoes, carrots, celery,
a turnip, and some I didn't even know the
names of.

Then I realized something. The singing
was coming from the turnip. I slowly
reached down and picked it up.

It stopped singing and screamed! I
dropped it like a hot potato. Or a cold
turnip.

I screamed, too. So we were both
screaming. Me and the turnip. I stopped
first and bent down to get a closer look. I
got the shock of my life. The turnip seemed

to have a face—what looked like two turnip eyes, a turnip nose, and a turnip mouth. It also had what looked like dark hair, combed straight back. And long sideburns. The lips on its turnip mouth were very full. The top lip looked higher on one side than the other. The lips looked like they were sneering. The turnip looked exactly like...Elvis Presley!

Chapter 2

The tabloid papers in the supermarket were right! Elvis had come back from the dead. As a turnip! And he was hanging out in my dad's vegetable bin.

The turnip had calmed down by now. So I picked it up from the kitchen floor.

"Mercy!" said the turnip. "Who are you?"

"My name's Zack," I answered. "Who are *you*?"

"Folks call me a lotta things, son," said the turnip. "But Ah answer to the name of Elvis."

"Why are you in my dad's vegetable bin?"

"Because Ah'm a vegetable, son. That's where us vegetables take care of business."

"Before you were a turnip, were you a world-famous singer?"

"No, son. Before Ah was a turnip, Ah was just a little ol' turnip seed in Tennessee."

"You mean you're not Elvis Presley, come back from the dead?"

"No, son. Ah'm Elvis the turnip, and Ah've come from the vegetable store on the corner. Your daddy bought me this morning."

"But you look just like Elvis Presley. And you were singing 'You Ain't Nothin' but a Hound Dog.'"

"Son, not everybody who looks like Elvis and sings 'You Ain't Nothin' but a Hound

Dog' is Elvis. Have y'all been to Las Vegas?"

"No. Why?"

"Son, half the people in Vegas look like Elvis and sing 'You Ain't Nothin' but a Hound Dog.'"

I stared at the talking turnip. I shook my head.

"Boy," I said. "This is quite a shock for me to find a singing turnip in my vegetable bin."

"Beggin' your pardon, son," said the turnip. "But it's a shock for me, likewise. Bein' yanked out of bed in the middle of the night. Ah was sleepin' like a baby."

"No you weren't," I said. "You were singing."

"Sometimes Ah sing in mah sleep," said the turnip.

"I've never heard of anybody singing in their sleep," I said.

"Have y'all heard of sleepwalkers, son?"

"Sure."

"Well, Ah'm a sleep*singer*. Speaking of which, Ah'm really bushed. Would y'all mind if Ah went back to sleep?"

"I guess not," I said.

"Son, would you promise me somethin'?"

"What?"

"Promise me y'all won't tell nobody 'bout me. Ah don't wanna wake up one mornin' and see mahself on the front page of *The National Enquirer*."

"Whatever you say, Elvis," I said.

"Ah'd appreciate that, son," he said.

"Anything else I can do for you?" I asked. "Would you like some other turnips for company?"

"You know what Ah'd really like?" said the turnip.

"What?"

"Ah'd like to have me a look around New

York City, son. See the sights. If that ain't too much trouble."

"Sure," I said.

"Ah'd be much obliged," said the turnip. "Ah'd also like to see Graceland."

"Elvis's home?" I said.

"Yep."

"I think that's in Memphis, Tennessee," I said. "That's like fifty thousand miles from here."

"Well, maybe some other time," said the turnip.

As I ate my cookies and drank my soda, Elvis told me more about his days growing up as a country turnip in Tennessee. When I finished my snack, I said good night. I tucked him in bed inside the vegetable bin and tiptoed back to my room.

I still couldn't believe it. Elvis was in the vegetable bin in Dad's refrigerator. OK, so maybe he wasn't the King himself. Just a turnip who looked and sounded almost exactly like him.

As I fell back asleep, I could hear far-off singing. At first I couldn't make out what it was, but then it came to me.

It was "Love Me Tender."

Chapter 3

The next morning I woke up to a terrible sound. Terrible, but somehow familiar. At first I couldn't think what it was. And then I knew.

It was the sound of a turnip screaming.

I raced into the kitchen.

Dad was standing at the counter in his pajamas. He was wearing headphones and listening to his Walkman. He had just turned on the electric juicer.

On the counter were some carrots, some celery, some vegetables I didn't recognize, and Elvis the turnip. Poor Elvis was scream-ing his lungs out. Well, I don't know if turnips have lungs. But if they do, he was screaming his out. Dad was getting ready to toss Elvis into the juicer!

"Help!" yelled the turnip. "Don't be cruel!"

"Dad!" I shouted. "Stop!"

Dad couldn't hear me either. He picked up Elvis and prepared to throw him in.

"Dad!" I shouted again. "Please stop!"

"Ah'm all shook up here!" yelled the turnip.

I dove for the wall outlet. I pulled the plug on the juicer just as Dad plopped Elvis into it.

"Zack!" said Dad. He looked startled. He took off his headphones. "What are you doing?"

"What are *you* doing?" I asked

"Making us some vegetable juice," he

said. "Why the heck did you yank the plug out of the wall?"

He started to put the plug back in.

"No, Dad! Stop!" I said. "You'll kill Elvis!"

"What?" said Dad.

"You threw Elvis in the juicer," I said. "If you turn it on, you'll kill him!"

"Elvis?" Dad frowned. He reached out and felt my forehead. "You seem a little feverish," he said. "Wait here. I'll get the thermometer."

"Dad, listen to me. I'm not feverish. I'm not sick. I'm just trying to save Elvis's life!"

"You can't do that," said Dad.

"Why not?"

"Elvis has been dead for more than twenty years."

"Not *that* Elvis," I said. "Not the Elvis the *singer*. Elvis the *turnip*. Didn't you hear him screaming?"

The frown returned to Dad's face. He started toward the bathroom again.

"Don't tell me you're not feverish, Zack," he said. "I know when you're feverish."

"Dad, listen to me!" I said. I reached into the juicer and pulled Elvis out. He was covered in carrot goo. The turnip kissed my hand. "This is no ordinary turnip," I said. "This turnip has a name. His name is Elvis."

Dad stopped and stared at me.

"I see," said Dad. He reached for a carrot and held it up. "What's the carrot's name—Skippy?"

"Dad, I'm serious. The turnip's name is Elvis. We met last night. He can talk and sing and everything. You can't make juice out of him!"

Dad burst into laughter.

"Dad, I'm not kidding," I said in my most serious voice. "We've seen some really strange stuff together. Poltergeists. Alternate universes on the other side of the medicine cabinet. An angry volcano goddess. You've seen me turning into a cat. You've seen me become invisible, OK? Why won't you believe this turnip can sing?"

I wiped the carrot goo off Elvis and shoved him in front of Dad's face.

"See? Doesn't he look like Elvis?"

Dad sighed.

"OK, I admit there's a resemblance," said Dad. "But I'm still not convinced. Have him sing me something."

I turned to the turnip.

"Sing something for my dad," I said.

The turnip didn't make a sound.

"I'm listening," said Dad, "but I'm not hearing."

"I don't think Elvis wants people to know he can sing," I said.

"If he doesn't start singing before I count

to ten," said Dad, "he's going to be juice. One…two…three…four…"

"Since mah baby left me, well Ah found a new place to dwell." The turnip really belted out the first verse of "Heartbreak Hotel." His eyes were skroonched shut. His forehead was wrinkled. His upper lip was drawn up.

Dad grabbed the counter to steady himself. He's seen a lot of weird things with me, but a turnip singing "Heartbreak Hotel" was right up there.

When Elvis was through singing, I applauded.

"Very nice, Elvis!" I said. "Very very nice!"

"Thankya. Thankya very much," said the turnip softly. He sounded exactly like the King.

Chapter 4

After Dad calmed down, he and Elvis and I had a nice talk. Elvis seemed really excited about seeing some sights in New York City. He'd never been out of Tennessee before. Elvis seemed most interested in going to the Hard Rock Cafe. He heard they had the other Elvis's jumpsuit from the movie *Viva Las Vegas*.

So around lunchtime, Elvis and I said good-bye to Dad. Then we headed out to the Hard Rock Cafe.

I don't know if you've ever been to the Hard Rock Cafe. The best part about it for me is the Cadillac. There's the rear end of a Cadillac sticking out of the wall above the front door. The Cadillac has these great tail fins. It looks as if it flew through the air and crashed into the Hard Rock Cafe. I love that. Don't ask me why. I just do.

There was a long line to get in. But the guy guarding the door took one look at Elvis and let us in right away.

Elvis really liked the Hard Rock Cafe. He loved the guitars on the wall, and the gold records and memorabilia from rock stars. Memorabilia means things that remind you of people. Stuff they owned, or stuff with their name on it. And we spent a long time in front of the glass case with Elvis Presley's jumpsuit from *Viva Las Vegas*.

Then we got called to our table.

I was so sick of health food, I ordered a big greasy cheeseburger with bacon and onions. Also a chocolate shake and a double order of fries. Elvis didn't order anything. He just sat on the table and watched me eat. Probably turnips don't eat food as we know it.

Just as I took the first big bite of my burger, a man came over to our table. He had dark hair and long sideburns. He had on a white vinyl jumpsuit with rhinestones all over it. The man's pants were bellbottoms. He wore a cape. Besides Superman, you don't see too many people wearing capes these days.

"Hello there, young fella," he said to me.

"Hi," I said. I wasn't too thrilled about talking to strangers, if you want to know the truth. Especially to weird-looking guys with capes.

"Allow me to introduce myself," he said.

"My name is Colonel Billy Bob Washburn. I happen to be the world's biggest collector of Elvis memorabilia."

"That's nice," I said. I wasn't being sarcastic. I really thought it was nice.

"If it has anything to do with Elvis," said the Colonel, "I got it. I got a quart of gas from a filling station Elvis worked in as a boy. I got the receiver of a telephone Elvis once talked into. I got a diner menu he once sneezed on."

"Cool," I said.

"I got an actual hair from Elvis's left sideburn. I got another hair from Elvis's right nostril."

"Hmm," I said. He was starting to gross me out.

"I got a toothpick Elvis used once, with a tiny speck of chicken-fried steak still on the tip of it. I got a pair of shoes worn by a fan that Elvis puked on."

Suddenly, my burger wasn't looking so tasty anymore.

"I couldn't help noticing the turnip," said the Colonel. "That turnip is the spitting image of the King himself."

"I know," I said. And I smiled at Elvis the turnip.

"I'd like to buy that turnip from you, son," said the Colonel. "I'll pay you eight hundred dollars for it."

Elvis looked outraged.

"The turnip isn't for sale," I said.

"I'll give you eleven thousand," said the Colonel, "but not a penny more."

Whoa! This guy was talking big bucks. But I just shook my head. I mean, who did he think he was anyway? To me, Elvis was more than a vegetable with a famous face. I wasn't about to let somebody stick him in a display case next to some Elvis Jockey shorts.

"I told you," I said. "The turnip isn't for sale. He's my friend."

"Kid, you drive a hard bargain," said the Colonel. He stared at me for a long moment. "I'll give you twenty-one thousand," he said. "But that's my final offer."

"Colonel Washburn, I already told you. The turnip's not for sale."

"Twenty-six," said the Colonel.

A waiter came over.

"Is this guy bothering you?" he asked.

"Maybe a little," I said.

"Twenty-seven five," said the Colonel.

"Leave this boy alone, buddy," said the waiter.

"I never take no for an answer," said the Colonel. "The word no has absolutely no meaning for me."

"Leave this boy alone, buddy, or you're out of here," said the waiter.

"I looked up the word no in the dictionary," said the Colonel. "And I *still* don't know what it means."

"That's it," said the waiter. "I'm calling the cops."

"I'm going, I'm going," said the Colonel. "But I want that turnip, kid. And what I want, I get. One way or another." And he left with a sweep of his cape.

That really gave me the willies. Elvis, too.

"Son," said Elvis, "if I had skin, I'd have goose pimples now."

I know I sure did.

On the way home I noticed a strange car about half a block back. It was a pink Cadillac with tail fins. I'd never seen anything like it. Except the one sticking out of the Hard Rock Cafe, I mean.

The weird thing about this Cadillac was that it went wherever I did. When I turned left down a side street, the pink Caddie did, too. When I stopped to wait for a light, the Caddie did, too—half a block away. When I got lost and went around the same block twice, so did the Caddie. No doubt about it, the pink Cadillac was definitely following me!

Chapter 5

When we got back to the apartment, Dad was pretty excited.

"Zack, do you realize what Elvis is?" he said.

"A singing turnip?" I asked.

"A gold mine!" said Dad.

"What do you mean?" I said.

"Do you realize how big this could be? An Elvis impersonator who's a turnip? I'll write his autobiography. It'll be a huge best-seller! Huge! We start by putting him on the David Letterman show. You know how David Letterman has a part of his show called Stupid Pet Tricks? We'll have him do Stupid *Vegetable* Tricks. Maybe we can even get Elvis his own TV talk show!"

"Elvis is a very private vegetable," I said. Elvis nodded. "He doesn't want that kind of life."

Dad turned to the turnip for the first time.

"Is that true?" Dad asked.

"Ah think so," said the turnip. "Sir, Ah'm kinda mixed up. Part of me wants to be alone with my thoughts and my music. But another part wants platinum records and Grammies. Beggin' your pardon, but why should Ah go on TV?"

"Well, for one thing," said Dad, "you'd have a chance to tell the world your message. What *is* your message, by the way?"

"Ah don't rightly know, sir," said the turnip. "Do Ah need a message?"

"Isn't there anything you want to tell mankind?" I asked.

"Like what, son?"

"Like 'Vegetables have feelings, too—don't eat us,'" I suggested. "Like 'Vegetarians are animals. They claim to be so sensitive, not eating meat. But they're cruel to poor defenseless salads.'"

Dad glared at me.

"I hope you're not going to use this as an excuse to stop eating your vegetables," said Dad.

"Dad," I said, "how could I ever eat another vegetable? After meeting Elvis? C'mon."

"You're telling me all vegetables talk and sing, just like Elvis?"

"Sure," I said. I got a carrot from the fridge. "Elvis, what's your carrot buddy's name?"

"That carrot don't have a name, son," said the turnip.

"But he talks, doesn't he?" I said. "I mean, you're buddies, aren't you? You and the carrots and the celery? You've been up most of the night, talking to them. Just like on a sleep-over, right?"

The turnip sighed. I'd never heard a turnip sigh before.

"Not to brag, son," said the turnip. "But ain't nobody in the bin can think, besides me. The others are just vegetatin'. In fact, Ah ain't had nobody to talk to for quite a spell...before you, that is."

"Where did you learn to talk?" Dad asked.

"Ah don't rightly know," said the turnip. "From the time Ah was a little ol' seedling on the farm in Tennessee, Ah just had this gift."

"And that's where you learned to sing?" Dad asked.

"Yes, sir," said the turnip. "The farmhands played the radio all day long. Mostly Elvis songs. 'Jailhouse Rock.' 'Love Me Tender.' 'Let Me Be Your Teddy Bear.' After a spell, Ah started hummin' along. And the rest is history."

"Well, Elvis," said Dad, "I'd say at least part of you wants a career in singing. Why not go to the Letterman show and audition?"

Elvis skroonched up his eyes and thought about that for awhile.

"Sir," said the turnip, "if y'all really think Ah should, then Ah guess it don't bother me none." Elvis smiled, and you could see from that smile why the world loved the King so much. "All right, let's do it," said Elvis the turnip.

Chapter 6

Dad had once done an article in *TV Guide* about the Letterman show, so he had connections there. He arranged for a tryout with one of their talent people. Her name was Stephanie Rozalsky. Elvis, Dad, and I took a cab to the Letterman office. I wasn't sure, but I thought I saw a Cadillac following us. A pink one.

Stephanie Rozalsky sat behind a big desk stacked with videotapes. She wore tiny round sunglasses with purple lenses. She had her hair in dreadlocks. There were photos of famous people all over her walls. I didn't know most of them. But I did recognize Shaquille O'Neal and Big Bird.

"So," said Stephanie. "I hear you have quite a gimmick. A turnip that appears to sing. Which one of you guys is the ventriloquist?"

"No ventriloquists," I said. "The turnip really sings."

"Right," said Stephanie. "And Barney is a real dinosaur."

"I can't speak for Barney," I said. "But the turnip really sings."

"Whatever you say," said Stephanie. "OK, let's see it."

I took Elvis out of my pocket.

"Whew!" said Stephanie. "He really does look like Elvis. The sideburns! The sneer! The cape!"

"I know," I said.

The cape was my idea. Dad and I made it out of a piece of white silk.

"All right," she said. "Let's hear him sing."

I turned to the turnip.

"Elvis," I said, "you're on."

The turnip didn't make a sound.

"Go on, Elvis," I said. "Sing!"

No sound of any kind came from the turnip.

"This is a put-on, right?" said Stephanie. She was smiling.

"No, no," I said. "It's not a put-on. I swear."

"You don't understand," said Stephanie. "We *like* put-ons at the Letterman show. In fact, we *love* put-ons. I think we can use this. It's a great act."

"But the turnip really sings," said Dad.

"Perfect," said Stephanie. "I love it! Say that when you're on the show."

Just then the turnip began to sing.

"Love me tender, love me true, all my dreams fulfill..." he sang.

Stephanie's eyes popped out so far they almost knocked her little purple sunglasses right off her nose. Then she started laughing so hard I thought she was going to choke. Finally she stopped laughing and dried her eyes.

"I don't know how you're pulling that stunt off," she said. "But it's great. Can you be on the show tonight? The President is supposed to come on, but I'll bump him."

"You'd bump the President of the United States to put on Elvis the turnip?" I asked.

"This is a much better act," said Stephanie. She led us out of her office. "Be in the greenroom at six-thirty."

As we left, we could still hear her chuckling. "Elvis is now leaving the building," I heard her say.

Chapter 7

We were so excited about the Letterman show, we were all ready by five o'clock. Dad and I dressed up like Elvis for the show. We rented Elvis wigs and suits from a costume place. Dad had on a black leather jumpsuit. I had on a metallic gold one. Mine was kind of big on me. And the wig itched.

On the way over in a cab, I thought I saw a pink Cadillac following us. But once we got to the theater, I forgot about it. I was going to be on a major network show, after all. It was easy finding the greenroom. It was a room backstage where all the guests waited who were going to be on the show. We heard Snoop Doggy Dogg was going to be on, too.

"Snoop Doggy Dogg is a rap singer," I told the turnip.

"If he's a hound dog, Ah'd sure like to meet him," said the turnip.

"No, no, he's a person," I said. "Dogs don't sing." Then I realized how dumb that must have sounded to a turnip who could sing.

One of the other guests was Dr. Phyllis, the famous psychologist. She was sitting on the sofa next to me. She was really little—her feet didn't even touch the floor. She was about the age of my Grandma Leah in Chicago. In fact, she reminded me of my Grandma Leah a lot.

"What are you going to be doing on the show, dear?" Dr. Phyllis asked me.

"I'm going to introduce Elvis the turnip," I said. "He's going to sing."

"I see," she said. "What does he sing?"

"Mostly old favorites like 'You Ain't Nothin' but a Hound Dog.'"

"You know," she said, "I have never heard of a turnip singing."

"You don't believe he sings?" I said.

"I believe anything you want to tell me, dear," she said gently. "I'm a psychologist."

"Ma'am," said the turnip, "Ah also sing 'Let Me Be Your Teddy Bear.' And Ah'm figurin' to do 'Viva Las Vegas' on the show tonight."

Dr. Phyllis stared at the turnip a moment.

"And how does that make you feel?" she asked him.

"Kinda nervous, ma'am," said the turnip. "See, Ah ain't never performed on TV before. Ah sure do hope Ah don't get stage fright and freeze up."

"Maybe I can help you with your nerves," said Dr. Phyllis. "As I said, I'm a psychologist. I help people with their problems."

"Pardon me for askin', ma'am," said the turnip. "But what do y'all charge?"

"Tonight I wouldn't charge you anything," said Dr. Phyllis. "But in my office I get two hundred dollars an hour."

"Mercy!" said the turnip.

"You know, Elvis," said Dr. Phyllis. "I don't get to talk to many turnips in my profession."

"Beggin you pardon, ma'am," said the turnip, "but at those prices, Ah ain't surprised."

I looked at the clock. It was almost time for us to go on. I was getting really nervous now about being onstage. In fact, I was sweating like crazy under my Elvis wig. I asked Dad to help me find the men's room.

I needed to splash some cold water on my face.

We left Elvis on the sofa with Dr. Phyllis. We got back to the greenroom just as Stephanie rushed in.

"OK, Elvis and friends," she said, "we're ready for you in makeup now." Stephanie stopped. "Hey, where *is* Elvis?"

I looked around. I didn't see Elvis anywhere. Dr. Phyllis was on the sofa, reading a magazine.

"Dr. Phyllis," I said. "Do you know where Elvis is?"

"Well, he told me he was feeling a little antsy," she said. "I think he might have walked outside for a breath of fresh air."

"Elvis couldn't have walked anywhere," I said. "He doesn't have feet."

"Oh no, dear. I don't mean the turnip," said Dr. Phyllis. "I mean the man in the white cape with the rhinestone collar and those big dark sunglasses."

A white cape? Rhinestones? Big dark sunglasses? Uh-oh, I remembered the pesty guy from the Hard Rock Cafe. Suddenly I realized who was inside the pink Cadillac I'd been seeing. Colonel Billy Bob Washburn. And, in a flash, I knew—Elvis had been kidnapped!

Chapter 8

"Poor Elvis!" I cried. "I've got to go find him!"

I jumped up and ran for the door. Stephanie grabbed me by my huge collar. She looked kind of upset.

"I'll tell you where you're going," she said. "On stage! You're booked on the Letterman show. And you're going on, with or without the turnip."

She stalked out of the room.

When she came back she shoved a yellow squash into my hand.

"Here! This was going to be dinner tonight," she said. "Meet your new Elvis!" Stephanie had scribbled a face and sideburns on the squash with a black felt-tip marker. She had tied a napkin around its neck for a cape. It was a sad excuse for my friend, Elvis the turnip. But before I could object, Stephanie pushed me and Dad out of the greenroom and onto the stage.

The lights onstage were a lot brighter than I thought they'd be. The audience was huge. For a minute, I was afraid I was going to totally freeze up. The only good thing about my stage fright was that it took my mind off poor Elvis the turnip.

"My next guests," said Mr. Letterman, "are a boy and his dad and their singing *squash*. The squash, ladies and gentleman, is an Elvis impersonator."

Mr. Letterman rolled his eyes. The audience laughed.

"Let's have a big welcome for Zack, his dad, and...Elvis the squash!" said Mr. Letterman.

There was a huge burst of applause. Dad pointed me to the sofa near Mr. Letterman's desk, and we sat down. The minute we did that, I felt better.

"So," said Mr. Letterman, "this is Elvis the singing squash."

"Right," said Dad.

"And he's an Elvis impersonator," said Mr. Letterman.

"Right," I said.

"And what is Elvis the singing squash going to perform for us tonight?" said Mr. Letterman.

"'All Shook Up,'" I said.

Mr. Letterman looked at the audience. He rolled his eyes. The audience laughed.

"All right, then," said Mr. Letterman.

"Ladies and gentleman, I give you Elvis the singing squash, singing 'All Shook Up.'"

The band played the introduction to "All Shook Up." The squash, of course, didn't sing. The band stopped playing.

"I thought the squash was going to sing," said Mr. Letterman.

"I thought so, too." I said. "I guess he has stage fright. He's all shook up."

The audience laughed. Mr. Letterman laughed.

"Ladies and gentleman," said Mr. Letterman. "This is the stupidest Stupid Vegetable Trick I've ever seen."

The audience laughed. Then they applauded.

"We'll be right back with Snoop Doggy Dogg," said Mr. Letterman.

Chapter 9

The second I got offstage I ran to the studio entrance. A security guard was standing there.

"Excuse me, sir," I said. "Did you happen to see a man with a turnip?"

"Big guy with a cape? And a white leather jumpsuit?" he asked.

"Actually, I think it was vinyl," I said. "But, yeah, that's him! He's a thief! A kidnapper! He stole Elvis the turnip!"

"Well, we can't let him get away with that," said the guard. "I'll call the police."

He took out a cell phone. "The guy in the cape was driving a pink Cadillac. They shouldn't have too much trouble finding him in that."

Just then Dad and Stephanie ran up.

"What's going on, Zack?" said Dad.

I told them about the Colonel and his weird obsession with Elvis. I told them the Colonel had kidnapped our poor turnip friend.

"Hey," said Stephanie, "the squash was a hit. So why worry about the turnip?"

"The turnip happens to be my friend," I said.

The security guard clicked his phone shut and turned back to us.

"The police have put out an APB on the pink Caddie," he said. "They're sending over an officer to write a report."

Officer Parsley showed up a few minutes later. He had long dark sideburns. It turned out he was a big Elvis fan, too. He offered to drive us around the city, looking for the Colonel. So Dad and I hopped in his cop car.

We'd barely pulled away from the curb when a call came in over the radio. Elvis the turnip had been found!

"Well, that wasn't too tough," said Officer Parsley. "I guess a pink Cadillac in New York sticks out like a pig in a cat show."

The cops had Elvis back at the station. He was really glad to see us. The cops loved him. He was singing them all of his songs. He had dedicated a special version of "Jailhouse Rock" to the guys who'd rescued him.

They had the Colonel in a cell in the back.

"That was really mean of you, Colonel," I said, "to kidnap poor Elvis. Why did you do it?"

"I told you, kid. I wanted that turnip. And what I want, I get. I just don't know the

meaning of the word no. I also don't know
the meaning of the word smorgasbord, but
that's another story. Tell me, kid, does the
turnip live with you?"

"He's staying with us for awhile," I said.
"Why do you ask?"

"If you have any personal things of his,"
said the Colonel, "I'd be glad to buy them
from you. Anything he wore. Anything he
handled or touched. Anything he looked at.
I'll pay top dollar."

"Forget it," I said.

"I mean it. Top dollar. Anything at all.
Name your price."

"I'm leaving now," I said.

We took Elvis home. At Dad's place I gave
the turnip a big hug.

"Elvis, I'm so glad to have you back," I
said. "I was really worried about you."

Elvis gave me a lopsided smile. "It wasn't
all that bad, son." he said. "And Ah even

got to see the Statue of Liberty from the back of the Cadillac."

"You know," I said, "I doubt they can keep the Colonel locked up for long on a charge of vegetable-napping. And he knows where we live. I'm afraid it isn't safe for you to stay here anymore."

"That's all right, son," said Elvis. "What Ah really want to do is to go to Graceland. That's been my lifelong dream. In fact, Ah'd like to spend the rest of my days planted in the Graceland vegetable garden."

So that's what happened. Dad and Elvis and I flew to Memphis, Tennessee. We paid for the plane tickets with the money we got for being on the Letterman show.

Elvis had never been on a plane before. He really liked it. He stayed on my tray table the whole trip. He kept staring out the window. I bet he was daydreaming about

Graceland. I had to watch that the flight attendant didn't clear him away with my dinner tray.

So Dad and I took Elvis to Graceland. Elvis was very impressed with the place. So were we, by the way. Dad and I got permission to plant Elvis in the Graceland vegetable garden. Then we said good-bye. Elvis promised to keep in touch.

We didn't hear anything from Elvis for a long time. I was beginning to get a little worried about him.

And then one day the mailman delivered a small package. It was addressed to me. There was no return address, but it had a Tennessee postmark.

I opened the package. Inside was an audio cassette. I put it in Dad's Walkman. It was "Let Me Be Your Teddy Bear." The voice was definitely the voice of a turnip.

And then I knew that Elvis was OK.